Sweet 'n' Slow

Apple Butter, Cane Molasses, and Sorghum Syrup Recipes

Patricia B. Mitchell

Copyright © 1988, 1989, 1992 by Patricia B. Mitchell.

Published 1992 by the author at the
Sims-Mitchell House Bed & Breakfast,
P. O. Box 429, Chatham, VA 24531.
   Tel/fax: 804-432-0595
   E-mail: answers@foodhistory.com
   Website: www.foodhistory.com

Printed in the U. S. A.
ISBN 0-925117-62-5

Sixth Printing, September 2000

- *Illustrations* -

Front Cover - **Stirring Apple Butter As It Cooks** *(see p. 3) and* **Feeding Sorghum Into the Mill** *(see pp. 13-14) by Henry H. Mitchell.*

Inside Title Page - **One-Horsepower Sorghum Mill** *(see pp. 13-14) by Henry H. Mitchell.*

Inside Back Cover - *portrait of the author by David L. Mitchell.*

Back Cover - *adapted from illustrations provided by Dover Publications, Inc., New York.*

Table of Contents

Introduction..1
Old Fashioned Apple Butter...................................1
Lula's Apple Butter..2
Spiced Apple Butter..3
Easy Apple Butter..4
Candy Apple Butter...4
Apple Butter Muffins...5
Moist Apple Butter Bread.....................................5
Golden Raisin, Pecan, & Apple Bread..........................6
ABC Apple Butter Cookies.....................................7
Topping Treats...7
    Daybreak Delight Duo Spread.........................7
    Molasses Sauce......................................8
    Creamy Citrus Spread................................8
    Molasses Butter.....................................8
Soppin' Sorghum..9
St. Charles Corn Bread......................................10
Pain au Sirop...10
Warm-Hearted Oat Loaf Bread.................................11
Soft Touch Molasses Bread...................................11
Molasses Banana Bread.......................................12
Brown Bread Loaves..13
Autumn Days Brown Bread.....................................15
Granddad Charlie's Bran Bread...............................15
My Bran Bread...16
Sweet Wheat Bread...16
Power Bread...17
Caraway and Rye Muffins.....................................18
Soft 'n' Tender Molasses Muffins............................19
Apple Pandowdy..20
"Gone Are the Days" Molasses Pie............................21
Molasses Raisin Pie...21
Molasses Crumb Pie..22
Shoo-Fly Pie..22
Egg-Free Pumpkin Pie..24
Indian Pudding..24
Sweet Potato Pudding..25
World War II Plum Pudding...................................26

Old Days Molasses Pudding.................................27
Old Home Place Molasses Oatmeal Cake...................27
Whittle Street Lemon Sauce....................................28
Creole Ginger Cake *("Gateau à la Melasse")*..............29
Second Helpin' Gingerbread...................................30
Great-Grandmère's Molasses Cookies......................30
Wheat Germ and Oatmeal Cookies..........................31
Sunny Oatmeal Cookies from Merry Lea..................31
So Fine Molasses Cookies.....................................32
Ginger Cookies...33
Ginger Wafers..33
Molasses Taffy...33
A Tug of the Heart..34
Molasses Popcorn Balls.......................................34
Maïs Tac-Tac...34
Butterscotch..35
Shaker Haying Water...35
Conclusion...36

Introduction

Imagine sweet, spicy mounds of apple butter spooned on hot biscuits or bread, and spread out like a rich frosting over the surface of that biscuit or slice of bread.... Bite into the morsel and taste the contrast of cool, lip-smacking apple butter and hot "staff of life." The full, fruity, floral aroma and taste of apples and the heady snap of spices make apple butter a "sauce" or spread that cannot be rivaled.

Next picture a semi-transparent trickle of golden brown sugar cane molasses being poured into the batter for a pan of satisfying, warm-from-the-oven gingerbread; or a lush stream of molasses coating the always-popular Cracker Jacks at the factory, or homemade sticky-good popcorn balls; or a hint of molasses adding just the right taste and savor to commercial Worcestershire Sauce.

Visualize slowly pouring spiraling threads of sorghum syrup onto steaming bowls of breakfast oatmeal or grits, or stacks of golden pancakes. Watch as the thick, dark brown liquid drips down the sides of the battercakes, pushing along with it yellow trails of melting butter. With your fork, cut into the stack of "culinary ecstasy" and sample the unique sweetness and piquancy of sorghum.

Are your gastric juices flowing now? Read on to discover more experiences with luscious apple butter, sugar cane molasses, and sorghum syrup.

Old-Fashioned Apple Butter

Apple butter is defined as "a kind of jam made from apples stewed with spices." The people of German ancestry known as the Pennsylvania Dutch are famous for making apple butter. Long ago, the recipes and instructions for this flavorful spread traveled with the Germans as they migrated from Pennsylvania and other parts of the northeast to places such as Old Salem, North Carolina. Nowadays apple butter is well-known and loved wherever there are apple orchards and

Germans. — In Wisconsin, Virginia, Tennessee, etc., there's a whole lot of "kettle stirring" going on!

* * *

6 lb. tart apples, cored and quartered (the prepared apples are known as "snits," a word probably originating through the Pennsylvania Dutch from the German word "schnitz," for "sliced" or "cut")
6 c. apple cider or apple juice
3 c. sugar
2 tsp. ground cinnamon
1 tsp. ground allspice (optional)
1/2 tsp. cloves

Cook apples and cider (or juice) in a large heavy saucepan until tender, about 30 minutes. Press through food mill. Boil gently 30 minutes, stirring often. Add sugar and spices. Cook, stirring, over low heat until sugar dissolves. Boil gently about 1 hour to desired thickness. Pour into hot 1/2-pint jars; adjust lids. Process in boiling water bath 10 minutes (start counting time after water returns to a boil). Makes 8 half-pints.

Lula's Apple Butter

My husband's Aunt Lula Mitchell Blankenship lives in White Gate, Bland County, Virginia. She has been making apple butter for decades. Here is her recipe, as written down by Mary Helvey Mitchell, my mother-in-law.

* * *

3 bushels cut apples (Leave on peelings; add water to cover; cook until tender.)

Put through a mill and cook until smooth. Add sugar to taste. Add vinegar (vinegar makes the apple butter smoother). Cook until thick. Add spices — oil of cloves, or cinnamon, or use together. Can in tins or glass.

* * *

    J. T. W. Mitchell, my father-in-law and Lula's brother, recalls his family's preparing apple butter in a kettle outside over a fire. (Mr. Mitchell was born around the turn of the century, and grew up in Bland County in southwest Virginia; Lula still lives in the "home place.") He says that they used apple cider to start cooking the apples in, rather than water. They peeled the apples in advance and kept adding more apples as they cooked down. The contents of the kettle had to be stirred continuously, using a long-handled flat paddle, to keep the apple mixture from scorching on the bottom. (Copper or brass 25-gallon capacity kettles are often used. The kettle must have smooth inner surfaces, and a somewhat rounded bottom is helpful so that the apples do not stick.) Required cooking time: eight hours or more! (The longer the apple butter cooks, the darker the color.)

Spiced Apple Butter

5 lbs. tart cooking apples, pared, cored, and quartered (about 12 cups)
3 c. apple cider
2 1/2 c. sugar (or to taste)
1 1/2 tsp. ground cinnamon
1/4 tsp. ground cloves

    Bring apples and cider to boiling point; cover and simmer 30 minutes. Puree apples in blender, adding sugar and spices. Pour into 13x9x2-inch baking dish and bake in 300° F. oven for two hours or until thick. Put in hot canning jars, leaving 1/4-inch headspace. Adjust lids and process in boiling water bath 10 minutes.

    - by Trudy Johnson, from **Idle Hens Don't Lay**, 1976, Woodlawn Academy, Chatham, VA.

Easy Apple Butter

To make a small quantity of apple butter with ease, use these instructions.

* * *

4 apples, peeled, cored, and chopped (Golden Delicious or Red Delicious or a mixture of the two are good choices for "city slickers" and those of us who do not normally have access to an orchard.)
1 c. water
1 1/2 tsp. cinnamon

Bring these three ingredients to a boil in a covered 1-quart saucepan. (Note: This recipe contains no sugar.) Uncover, reduce heat, and let simmer, stirring frequently. When apple chunks are quite tender and are easy to mash with a spoon, test for proper thickness by placing a spoonful on a plate. The apple butter is done when no watery ring forms around the edge. At this point, pour the apple butter into a blender and blend until smooth.

This spread will keep for several weeks in a covered container in the refrigerator. It also freezes well. Its taste is superb on toast, pancakes, and muffins.

Candy Apple Butter

To gratify the child that is in each of us, try this "rendition of the apple-butter song."

* * *

6 c. applesauce
5 c. sugar
1/4 c. vinegar
1/2 lb. cinnamon candy

Combine the ingredients in a saucepan. Bring to a boil. Cook 15-20 minutes, stirring often. Pour into jars and seal.

Apple Butter Muffins

My mother didn't can or preserve foods when I was a child, so we relied on store-bought products. Nevertheless, my fondness for apples and apple butter developed early. We had six apple trees in our yard, all of which bore fruit, albeit rather grudgingly. Wasps dined on a lot of the apples, but some were retrieved for Mom's out-of-this-world apple pie. Any apple flavor still thrills my palate. These Apple Butter Muffins will tingle your taste buds, too.

Incidentally, the J. M. Smucker Company of Orville, Ohio, started out pressing apple butter in 1897. Now they are the biggest jelly and jam manufacturer in the U. S. A.

* * *

1 egg
1 c. milk
1 c. all-purpose flour
1 c. whole wheat flour
4 tsp. baking powder
3/4 tsp. salt
2 tbsp. brown sugar, packed
1 c. raisins
2 tbsp. butter or margarine, melted
1/2 c. apple butter

Beat together egg and milk. In a separate container mix the dry ingredients. Combine these two mixtures. Blend in the melted butter and apple butter last. Spoon into 12 greased muffin cups and bake at 400° F. for around 20 minutes.

Moist Apple Butter Bread

Apple butter moistens and spices this delectable loaf. After baking, allow the loaf to sit overnight so that the flavors intermingle, and so that the loaf crumbles less when sliced.

This is one of my all-time-favorite bread recipes.

* * *

1 c. milk
1/3 c. vegetable oil
2 eggs, beaten
2 c. apple butter
2 c. bran (oat bran is also excellent)
1/2 c. brown sugar, packed
1 c. raisins
3 c. whole wheat flour
1 tbsp. baking powder
1 tsp. salt

Combine the first seven ingredients and let sit for five minutes. Add the last three ingredients, mix, and spoon into two greased 9x5-inch loaf pans. Bake at 350° F. for 45 minutes.

Yield: 2 loaves.

Note: You may substitute apple butter in bread or cake recipes which call for applesauce and cinnamon (and other "apple pie" - type spices — cloves, allspice, nutmeg). Just use an equal amount of apple butter in place of the applesauce, and omit the spices.

Golden Raisin, Pecan, & Apple Butter Bread

Irresistibly good, this quick loaf bread will make breakfast time as much fun as a birthday party. (The bread is better than cake!)

* * *

2 1/2 c. self-rising flour (or 2 1/2 c. plain flour, 1 tbsp. baking powder, and 1/2 tsp. salt)
2 tbsp. sugar
1 tsp. cinnamon (unless the apple butter is really spicy)
1/4 c. vegetable oil
3/4 c. apple butter

1/2 c. golden raisins
1 c. pecans, chopped
2 c. milk

Mix the dry ingredients. In a separate bowl combine the remaining ingredients, and then stir together the two mixtures. Spoon into a greased loaf pan and bake at 350° F. for around 50 minutes.

ABC Apple Butter Cookies

2 c. whole wheat flour
2 tsp. baking powder
1/2 tsp. salt
1 tsp. cinnamon
2 c. quick oats
1 c. nuts (walnuts or pecans), chopped
1/3 - 1/2 c. brown sugar, packed
2 tbsp. vegetable oil
2 c. apple butter
3/4 c. water

Mix dry ingredients. Add liquids. Mix, and drop spoonfuls on lightly-greased baking sheets. Bake at 350° F. for 15 minutes. Note that sugar and cinnamon may be varied according to taste, and based on the flavor of the apple butter used as an ingredient.

Topping Treats

The following four topping-treat selections are fun-to-eat toppings utilizing the "stars" of this book.

Daybreak Delight Duo Spread:

Fold cane or sorghum molasses into apple butter, peach jam, or cherry preserves, and serve with toast.

Molasses Sauce:

This topping is really great on pancakes!

1/4 c. butter
1/2 c. cane or sorghum molasses

Cream together ingredients and heat.

Creamy Citrus Spread:

Smooth and zesty, this bread spread will win compliments.

1 tbsp. cane or sorghum molasses
2 tsp. grated orange peel
1 8-oz. pkg. cream cheese

Cream together all ingredients. Chill. Serve as a spread for sweet bread (such as pumpkin, zucchini, brown bread, etc.).

Molasses Butter:

Settlers traveling west in the 1800's came up with this concoction. On the rare occasion that fresh cream became available on their journey, very often the motion of the wagon caused it to turn to butter! Here was one way to utilize that special butter:

1 c. cane or sorghum molasses
2 tbsp. butter
1/4 tsp. ground nutmeg
Dash of baking soda
2 eggs, well-beaten

Mix the first four ingredients in a saucepan. Bring to a boil. Stir a bit of hot mixture into eggs, then return a small portion to the saucepan. Gradually add the rest of the eggs. Cook 1 minute, until thick. Chill. Makes 1 1/2 cups.

Soppin' Sorghum

*The following slurpy description (from **North Carolina and Old Salem Cookery** (1955) by Elizabeth Hedgecock Sparks) sets the mood for cooking, eating, and just thinking about food.*

"*A cruet of sorghum or 'lasses was standard equipment on tables from early fall to late spring . . . . Sorghum is still made but the supply is limited. It appears in neighborhood grocery stores and at farmers' markets packed in fruit jars or jugs in late October or early November. Most of the sorghum will turn to sugar or will ferment with the warm spring weather. But with a family which loves to 'sop' the supply is gone long before warm weather arrives, and they begin looking forward to a new batch in the fall. Soppin' sorghum is rather an art — one based on the individual. Some folks begin by slicing off a big hunk of soft butter. Sorghum is poured over the butter and the two are stirred together. Big flecks of yellow butter mingle with the golden syrup. A hot biscuit is pushed around and around in this mixture until it is coated. Those who are dainty push the biscuit with a fork, but most often, the biscuit is hand pushed.*"

Georgia's founders promised any man, woman, or child who endured a year in the colony of Georgia a reward of 64 quarts of molasses!

Today we still enjoy the rewarding taste of cane molasses; and, in Virginia each autumn — as in many other places across the country — my family and I can taste and see the "cottage industry" of sorghum molasses extraction at the many events sponsored by schools, churches, and community groups at which fresh sorghum is made and sold. For example, both the Clifford (Amherst County) and Climax (Pittsylvania County) Ruritan Clubs conduct annual sorghum festivals.

St. Charles Corn Bread

The following is a 19th-century recipe from the St. Charles Hotel in New Orleans, recorded by Hugo Ziemann and Mrs. F. L. Gilette in *The White House Cookbook* (Saalfield Publishing Company, New York, 1915, p. 247).

* * *

2 c. sifted cornmeal
1/2 c. flour
2 c. sour milk
2 well-beaten eggs
1/2 c. molasses or sugar
1 tsp. salt
2 tbsp. melted butter

"Mix the meal and flour smoothly and gradually with the milk, then the butter, molasses and salt, then the beaten eggs, and lastly dissolve *a level teaspoonful of baking soda* in a little milk and beat thoroughly altogether. Bake nearly an hour in well-buttered tins, not very shallow. This recipe can be made with sweet milk by using baking powder in place of soda."

Pain au Sirop

"Take one loaf of stale bread (or cold biscuit[s] are better), and one quart of New Orleans molasses. Put the frying pan on the fire, with a lump of fresh butter the size of an egg. Cut the bread in slices as for toast, (or the biscuit in halves), soak in some of the molasses and put in the frying-pan when the butter is melted, pouring some molasses over it. Let it fry well on both sides, and when the molasses begins to candy it is done. Continue this until all the bread is used. Serve cold. It is better when twenty-four hours old."

- *The Spinning-Wheel Cookbook*, the Spinning-Wheel Club, Woodville, MS, 1899, reprinted by The Woodville Civic Club, Inc., 1983, p. 25.

Warm-Hearted Oat Loaf Bread

Cane molasses and sorghum molasses are nutritionally superior to sugar. Dark cane molasses, blackstrap molasses, and sorghum molasses are all good sources of iron. Phosphorus and calcium are also contained in these products.

Human nature being what it is, however, folks figured out how to take a healthful substance and make it into an unhealthful product, for cane molasses is a principal ingredient in rum. (Sorghum molasses could also purportedly make a mighty smooth and mellow rum!)

Historians estimate that before the Revolutionary War, colonists — including women and children — consumed an average of four gallons of rum per person per year. — The following nutritious bread recipe will utilize molasses in a way that benefits your body far more than "Demon Rum!"

* * *

1 1/2 c. quick oats
1 1/2 c. whole wheat flour
2 tsp. baking powder
1/8 - 1/4 tsp. salt
2 tsp. ginger
1/2 c. raisins
3/4 c. cottage cheese
1 1/4 - 1 1/3 c. milk
2 tbsp. vegetable oil
1/3 c. cane or sorghum molasses

Combine the dry ingredients. In a separate container mix the liquids. Stir together the two mixtures (adding the extra milk if needed), and spoon the batter into a greased 9x5-inch loaf pan. Bake in a preheated 350° F. oven for 40-45 minutes.

Soft Touch Molasses Bread

There are many grades of molasses, varying in content from 36% to 50% sugar. The purest is made for 100%

natural sugar cane juices, clarified, reduced, and blended. This is cane syrup. If a manufacturer wants sugar, he processes the cane juice by boiling it, extracting raw sugar and ending up with "left-over" cane liquid or juice — this is first extraction molasses. The first extraction molasses can be boiled again with water added so that more sugar can be extracted. This is "second extraction molasses" or simply "second molasses," and so on. The more times the liquid is boiled the less sweet it becomes because more sugar has been removed. After several boilings blackstrap molasses results. (This dark, strong syrup has an almost overpowering taste; and some devoted fans — my Dad loved it on toast or bread, and I do, too.)

First or second extraction molasses is fine for use in Soft Touch Molasses Bread. (An example of first extraction molasses is "*Grandma's* Green Label Molasses.")

* * *

3 1/4 c. whole wheat flour
2 tsp. baking soda
1/2 tsp. salt
2 c. buttermilk or sour milk
1/2 c. molasses

Mix dry ingredients. Mix liquids; stir into the dry ingredients, moistening completely. Spoon into a greased 9x5-inch loaf pan and bake at 350° F. for 40 minutes, or until a toothpick inserted in the loaf comes out dry. Makes 1 loaf.

Molasses Banana Bread

The following bread is delightful served warm at breakfast. (Bake ahead of time and re-heat!) The bananas add moistness.

* * *

3 c. whole wheat flour
1 1/2 tsp. baking soda
1 tsp. baking powder
1/4 tsp. salt
1 tsp. cinnamon
1/4 tsp. cloves
1/4 tsp. nutmeg
2 tbsp. brown sugar, packed
2 tbsp. vegetable oil
1/4 c. cane or sorghum molasses
2 large ripe bananas, mashed
1/2 c. nuts, chopped (walnuts or pecans are good)
1/2 c. raisins
1 3/4 c. milk

    Combine the first seven ingredients. In a separate bowl, mix the remaining ingredients. Combine the two mixtures. Spoon into a greased 9x5-inch loaf pan and bake at 350° F. for around 40 minutes or until the loaf tests done. (To check for doneness, insert a toothpick near the center of the loaf. If the toothpick comes out clean — with no sticky batter on it — the bread should be removed from the oven and set on a wire rack to cool. Don't fret if you have no wire rack; just put the bread on a surface that will not be damaged by heat. Cover with a clean towel or cloth napkin. Over that, loosely place a piece of clear plastic wrap. This keeps the bread from drying out.)

Brown Bread Loaves

    The making of sorghum molasses or syrup is a fascinating process to watch. In the autumn many community groups gather to make and sell the product, and suddenly a "festival" originates!

    Sorghum molasses is made by pressing the juice out of the stalks of a particular type of cereal grass (sorgos). Rollers are used to squeeze the liquid out of the stalks, and then the juice is boiled down to the desired thickness. (This might take 6-8 hours, or longer.) The procedure is usually done outdoors, and sometimes a mule or horse is used to power the old-fashioned cane mill. (The animal circles the mill and to him is attached a long pole called a "sweep" which powers the mill.) Sometimes the power take-off of a farm tractor is used as the power source for the mill. After the juice is squeezed, filtered, and boiled down, it is put into jars or jugs to enjoy. Incidentally, six acres of sorgos yield 60 tons of stripped cane (the usable stalks). From the stalks are squeezed about 360 gallons of juice, which is cooked down to 60 gallons of sorghum syrup or "'lasses."

Now, the following bread can be made with either sugar cane molasses or sorghum syrup. A satisfying stick-to-the-ribs recipe, it is grand served with baked beans, or with butter at breakfast.

I prepare loaf breads in my "spare time" (is there any such thing?), then freeze or refrigerate, and use as needed. — Actually, breadmaking is my hobby, so I consider it fun (not a chore). The reward of baking homemade bread is in serving it to others and eating it oneself.

* * *

3 1/2 c. whole wheat flour
1/2 c. sugar
2 tsp. baking soda
2 tsp. salt
1/2 c. cornmeal
1 egg
1/2 c. cane or sorghum molasses
2 c. milk
1/2 c. melted butter, margarine, or vegetable oil

Mix the dry ingredients. In another bowl, beat together the egg and liquids. Combine the two mixtures, and pour into two greased 9x5-inch bread pans. Bake at 325° F. for 50 minutes or until firm to the touch.

Yield: 2 loaves.

Autumn Days Brown Bread

Raisins liven up the next brown bread recipe.

* * *

2 c. whole wheat flour
1 c. unbleached flour
1 1/2 tsp. baking soda
1/2 tsp. salt
3/4 c. raisins
1/2 c. cane or sorghum molasses
1 3/4 c. buttermilk or sour milk (or thinned yogurt)

Combine the first five ingredients. In a separate bowl stir together the liquids. Combine the two mixtures, and spoon the batter into a greased 9x5-inch loaf pan. Bake at 350° F. for 55-60 minutes.

Following are two good and basic bran breads.

Granddad Charlie's Bran Bread

2 c. whole wheat flour
1 1/2 c. bran
1 tbsp. baking powder
1/2 tsp. salt
2 tbsp. vegetable oil
1/3 c. cane or sorghum molasses
1 2/3 c. milk

Stir together the dry ingredients. Mix liquids. Combine the two mixtures, stirring to moisten completely. Spoon the batter into a greased bread pan, and bake at 350° F. for 35-40 minutes, or until a toothpick inserted near the center comes out clean.

My Bran Bread

Just a "jerp" of molasses sweetens this bread. Bill Neal, in his *Biscuits, Spoonbread and Sweet Potato Pie* (Alfred A. Knopf, Inc., New York, 1990, p. 75) pointed out: "Sorghum was the poor man's sugar cane, the source of molasses for much of the South but it was known on every table, rich or poor."

* * *

2 1/2 c. whole wheat flour
1 1/2 c. bran or wheat germ
1/2 tsp. salt
1 1/2 tsp. baking soda
1/4 c. brown sugar, packed
1/2 c. raisins (optional)
1/4 c. cane or sorghum molasses
2 - 2 1/2 c. buttermilk or sour milk

Mix the dry ingredients. Combine the molasses and milk. Stir together the two mixtures and spoon into a greased 9x5-inch loaf pan. Bake at 350° F. for about 50 minutes.

Sweet Wheat Bread

Yeast bread is lots of fun to prepare, but be ready to practice patience — this yeast bread is not part of the microwave age. You must wait for the yeast to bubble and thicken and do its work. Do not try to rush things; just relax and enjoy the bread-making process.

These loaves are irresistibly soft and kissed with molasses flavor.

* * *

3 pkg. or 3 tbsp. baking yeast
1/2 c. warm water
1 c. honey
3 1/2 c. warm milk

1 c. water (preferably potato cooking water)
1/2 c. vegetable oil
3/4 c. cane or sorghum molasses
1 1/2 tbsp. salt
7 1/2 c. whole wheat flour
5 c. all-purpose, unbleached, or bread flour

Dissolve yeast in the 1/2 c. warm water with the 1 c. honey. When the mixture bubbles, mix in other ingredients. Knead long and hard. (This bread is worth the trouble! — I usually divide the dough into two or three parts to knead because it is too large an amount of dough to work with.) When well-kneaded, consolidate the dough and put it into a large greased bowl (or two, if you haven't a mammoth enough bowl). Let rise until doubled. Punch down, and form 4 loaves. Allow them to rise in greased loaf pans in a warm spot. When high enough, bake at 350° F. for 50 minutes.

Yield: 4 loaves.

Power Bread

This muscle bread is not for those with weak teeth or jaws, or timid taste buds. It's flavor-packed and vitamin-stacked. We are nutrition-conscious, especially when I'm "assembling a baby." I developed this "health-bread" during my second pregnancy, and our second child, David, is definitely full of get-up-and-go, so the bread must have helped!

* * *

2 pkg. or 2 tbsp. baking yeast
3 c. warm water
2/3 c. cane or sorghum molasses
1/3 c. vegetable oil
2 tsp. salt or kelp
1 1/3 c. dry milk powder
2 c. wheat germ
1 c. soy flour

1/2 c. brewer's yeast powder
1/4 c. lecithin granules
Whole wheat flour

Dissolve the yeast in the warm water with the molasses added. When the yeast froths up, add other things, using enough whole wheat flour to make a firm dough. Knead well, and place ball of dough in a greased bowl. Brush surface of dough with oil; cover with plastic wrap, and allow to rise in a warm place. Punch down. Form three loaves and place in greased loaf pans. Allow to rise until light. Bake at 350° F. for about 45 minutes.

Yield: 3 loaves.

Caraway and Rye Muffins

Columbus introduced sugar cane to the West Indies in 1493. Molasses became one of the most important products of the West Indies, and an integral part of colonial trade. It was, in fact, the major sweetener used in America until after World War I, when sugar prices dropped (causing people to buy more sugar).

If you use sorghum molasses in this recipe (or any other), be sure to select top-quality sorghum. The way to judge it is to sample a little bit straight. Sorghum connoisseurs assert that the ideal sorghum syrup is sweet, soft-flavored, and mellow, with no harsh "bite." (The bitterness associated with some sorghum syrup supposedly results from its being grown on unsuitable soil.)

Whether cane or sorghum molasses is used, these Caraway and Rye Muffins are an unusual flavor addition to breakfast, lunch, or dinner.

* * *

1 c. whole wheat flour
1 c. rye flour
1 tbsp. baking powder

1 tsp. salt
1/4 c. dry milk powder
1 tbsp. caraway seeds
2 eggs, beaten
1 c. milk
1/4 c. cane or sorghum molasses
2 tbsp. vegetable oil

Mix the first six ingredients. In a separate bowl, stir together the liquid ingredients. Combine the two mixtures and spoon into greased muffin tins. Bake at 375° F. for approximately 20 minutes.

Soft 'n' Tender Molasses Muffins

Some historians argue that the Molasses Act of 1733 played a greater role in precipitating the Revolutionary War than did the British tax on tea coming into American ports. The Molasses Act, mostly evaded by the colonists, levied a heavy tax on sugar and molasses coming from anywhere except the British sugar islands in the Caribbean.

In fact, it has been speculated that the restrictions placed on colonists' importation of sugar and cane molasses may have spurred on the colonies' production and use of sorghum as a sweetener.

Use either cane molasses (popular before the time of Christ in Arabia, India, and China) or sorghum molasses (long produced in southern Europe and China) to kiss these "gems" with delicate sweetness. You'll love their silky, smooth texture!

* * *

2 c. all-purpose, unbleached, or whole wheat flour
2 tsp. baking powder
1/2 tsp. salt
1/2 tsp. baking soda
1 egg, beaten
2 tbsp. vegetable oil

3/4 c. buttermilk or sour milk
1/2 c. cane or sorghum molasses

Sift together dry ingredients. In a different bowl, beat liquids together. Combine the mixtures. Pour into greased muffin cups. Bake at 400° F. for about 20 minutes.

Yield: 12 large muffins.

Apple Pandowdy

Guess where the adjective "dowdy" comes from! Yep, Apple Pandowdy. Nobody seems to remember the origin of the suffix "-dowdy," but some believe it might be from a word describing a deep pan as spoken in an ancient Somersetshire (England) dialect. Wherever the word originated, the top crust of this old-fashioned pie is chopped up; and as the years passed, this "messed-up" appearance came to be the definition of "dowdy."

* * *

Pastry for a 2-crust 9-inch pie (to be rolled out and used in a 13x9x2-inch baking dish)
1/4 c. butter, melted (Margarine can be used, but the flavor will, of course, be less rich and "authentic.")
1/2 c. sugar
1/2 tsp. ground cinnamon
1/4 tsp. ground nutmeg
Dash of salt
10 peeled and thinly-sliced medium-sized apples
1/2 c. cane or sorghum molasses
1/4 c. water
3 tbsp. butter, melted

Roll out the pie pastry to a 15x11-inch rectangle (approximately). Brush the dough with a tablespoon of butter, and then cut in half. Place the halves on top of each other, and brush with butter. Cut in half again. Repeat twice more, brushing with butter each time. Place all of the pieces on top of each other. Chill for 2 hours. Roll out the dough, and divide in half. Use half to line a greased 9x13x2-inch baking dish. In a bowl mix together the sugar, spices, and apples. Put into the pastry-lined dish. Combine the molasses, water, and melted butter, and pour over the apples. Cover with the remaining dough and seal edges. Bake at 400° F. for 10 minutes. Reduce the heat and bake at 325° F. for 30-40 minutes, or until the apples are tender. Remove from the oven and "dowdy" the crust by making slashes through the top crust with a sharp knife. Return to the oven for 10 more minutes. — Traditionally served hot with cream.

"Gone Are the Days" Molasses Pie

"One teacup of molasses, two eggs, one tablespoon of butter. Flavor with ginger." [Mix everything together and pour into an unbaked pie shell. Bake at 350° F. until firm.]

- ***The Spinning-Wheel Cookbook**, the Spinning-Wheel Club, Woodville, MS, 1899, reprinted by The Woodville Civic Club, Inc., 1983, p. 34.*

Molasses Raisin Pie

Mix in saucepan:

1/2 c. sugar
1 c. water
4 tbsp. flour
1 tsp. cinnamon
1 1/2 c. seedless raisins
1/2 c. molasses
1/2 tsp. salt
1 tbsp. lemon juice

Cook filling until thick. Cool. Pour into unbaked pie shell and bake 10 minutes at 450° F.; reduce heat to

350° F. for 30 minutes more. Serve plain or with whipped cream.

- *Recipes of the Early 1800's, Nathan Bedford Forrest Chapter UDC, Woodville, MS, 1985, p. 13.*

Molasses Crumb Pie

Mix:

1/2 c. molasses
1/2 tsp. baking soda, dissolved in 3/4 c. hot water
1 beaten egg yolk

Pour liquid into an unbaked pie crust.

Mix crumbs of:

3/4 c. flour
1/2 tsp. cinnamon
1/2 tsp. nutmeg
1/4 tsp. ginger
1/4 tsp. cloves
1/2 c. brown sugar
2 tbsp. butter
1/2 tsp. salt

Top liquid with crumbs (which have been well blended by hand). Bake at 400° F. for 10 minutes. Reduce heat to 325° F. Bake for 45 minutes or until firm.

Note: The crumb mixture above may be used as topping for other fruit pies, instead of a rolled top crust.

- *Recipes of the Early 1800's, p. 13.*

Shoo-Fly Pie

Among the Pennsylvania Dutch all the myriad of dishes, including sweet pies, of their incredibly big meals are set out on the table before the diners sit down. It is customary to partake of pie right along with the meats; vegetables; preserves; and condiments (the prescribed "seven sweets and seven sours"); and there are also cakes and cooked desserts like puddings, and sugar or fruit dumplings! No wonder the Amish are wont to say at mealtime, "Eat yourself full," and "Come in and shovel yourself out."

Popular pies, besides Shoo-Fly, are butterscotch, chocolate, custard, rhubarb, pumpkin, apple, berry, half-moon, mince, lemon, and "funeral pie" (a lemon-raisin pie traditionally baked when someone dies). — The name Shoo-Fly Pie is self explanatory; happily, we have window screens in this day and age!

Note: Sorghum or cane molasses works well in the following recipe provided by the Merry Lea Environmental Learning Center, Goshen College, Goshen, Indiana.

* * *

Bottom part:

3/4 c. cane or sorghum molasses
3/4 c. boiling water
1/2 tsp. baking soda

Dissolve soda in hot water and add molasses.

Crumb part:

1/4 c. shortening
1 1/2 c. flour
3/4 c. brown sugar, packed
Dash nutmeg and cinnamon

Combine sugar and flour and rub in shortening to make crumbs.

Put crumbs and liquid in alternating layers with crumbs on bottom and top in a 9-inch pie shell. Bake at 375° F. for approximately 35 minutes or until set.

Egg-Free Pumpkin Pie

In the 19th century the ingredients used to fill pie crusts were nicknamed "pie timber;" so assemble your pie timber, and bake up "a nice ol'-fashioned punkin' pie!" — This one is suitable even on the days when your hen won't lay!

* * *

2 unbaked pastry shells
4 c. cooked pumpkin, mashed
Milk to moisten
1/3 c. cane or sorghum molasses (or more to suit your sweet tooth)
1/2 tsp. salt
1 tbsp. ginger
1 tsp. cinnamon or nutmeg

Combine all ingredients (except the pie crusts!) and spoon into the unbaked pie shells. Bake at 350° F. for close to 40 minutes, checking for doneness by inserting a toothpick (or a *clean* broom straw or an uncooked spaghetti noodle!) into the custard-like filling. When the filling is set (not gooey) and the crust "golden brown" (as they say), remove from oven.

Indian Pudding

Indian Pudding is an old-timey, all-American dessert. Native Americans introduced early settlers to cornmeal, and being lovers of puddings, the English colonists soon learned to make an acceptable dessert which they sweetened with molasses. The following recipe is a slightly modernized version of a classic, courtesy of my friend Viola Laws, food historian at Old Bedford Village in Pennsylvania.

* * *

1/4 c. cornmeal
1 tsp. salt

1 c. water
2 c. milk
1 egg, beaten
1/4 c. sugar
1/2 c. molasses
1 tbsp. butter
1 tsp. cinnamon
1/2 tsp. ginger
1 c. cold milk

    Mix cornmeal, salt, water and milk in a saucepan. Boil gently 10 minutes, stirring constantly. Remove from fire and add egg, sugar, molasses, butter, cinnamon, and ginger. Pour into buttered baking dish and bake for 1/2 hour. Then stir in extra cup of milk and bake until brown.

Sweet Potato Pudding

    Grate (use grate or shredding blade of food processor) enough sweet potatoes to render 3 cups (if there is a little more, use it). Two large potatoes will probably be sufficient.

2 c. milk
3 or 4 eggs
1/3 c. melted butter
2 1/2 c. sugar
1/2 c. molasses
1/2 tsp. cinnamon
1/4 tsp. nutmeg (grated fresh!)
1/4 tsp. allspice
1 tsp. vanilla
1/2 tsp. salt

    Put all ingredients into a large mixing bowl. Mix and add grated potatoes. Bake at 425° F. until brown and crusty around the edges. (I usually bake in a buttered metal pan but a casserole can be used. This is a dessert but if you cut down on the sugar it is nice to use as a vegetable. Omit 1 cup sugar to use as a vegetable dish.)

*- Recipe courtesy Ginny Gordon,
Beaufort, North Carolina*

World War II Plum Pudding

Plum pudding is a traditional Christmas dessert, the English origins of which can be traced back more than 300 years. Back in the 1700's this steamed pudding probably actually contained plums, but over the passage of time currants and raisins became the favored ingredients. Suet is still used in this recipe. (Ask your butcher to grind some for you.) Plum pudding can be made months in advance and frozen. It is usually served warm with a dessert sauce. (I came across this surprising historical nugget in the *1857 Graham-Ginestra House Book One* from Rockford, Illinois: "Some cooks serve Brandy over the pudding, others use a butter sauce and some use turkey gravy [!!] over the pudding.")

The following plum pudding, dating from the World War II era, reflects a grim period in our nation's history during which the U. S. citizens on the home front, not fully recovered from the Great Depression, had to make sacrifices and "tighten their belts" even further. White refined sugar was rationed, as some of you will remember, so this recipe calls for molasses in place of sugar. No currants (the dried fruit of a small, seedless grape grown in the Mediterranean region, used in cooking) are required in this dish.

* * *

1 heaping c. bread crumbs
2 heaping c. flour
1 tsp. each baking soda, salt, cloves, cinnamon, nutmeg
1 c. suet, chopped finely
1 c. raisins

1 c. cane or sorghum molasses
1 c. milk

    Combine all ingredients, and boil, covered, for 2 1/2 hours in a 2-quart double boiler or a 2-quart pail set in a kettle of boiling water.

Old Days Molasses Pudding

    Sweet and easy! — You may wish to experiment with this heirloom recipe. It is rich and flavorful.

* * *

1 c. boiling water
1 tsp. baking soda
1/4 tsp. salt
1/2 c. butter
1 c. cane or sorghum molasses
1 c. brown sugar, packed
2 eggs, well-beaten
1 tsp. cinnamon
1 tsp. ginger
1 tsp. cloves

    Combine the ingredients in the order listed, and pour into a baking dish. Bake at 350° F. for 30 minutes, or until firm.

Old Home Place Molasses Oatmeal Cake

    Back in the 1830's, a bride's popularity was measured by the number of layers of molasses stack cake guests brought to her wedding reception. The following cake will make *you* popular! It is akin to gingerbread, but more moist. Serve with lemon sauce, a dollop of vanilla ice cream, or plain yogurt.

* * *

1 1/2 c. boiling water
1 c. quick-cooking oats
1/2 c. vegetable oil
3/4 c. cane or sorghum molasses
2 tbsp. honey
1 1/4 c. flour (all-purpose, unbleached, or whole wheat)
1 tsp. baking soda
2 tsp. baking powder
1/2 tsp. salt
1/2 tsp. cinnamon
1/2 tsp. ginger
1/4 tsp. cloves
1/4 tsp. nutmeg

Pour boiling water over oats. Stir and let sit 20 minutes. In a different bowl, combine oil, molasses, sugar, and eggs. Stir in oats mixture. Sift dry ingredients, and gradually add to wet mixture. Combine thoroughly. Pour batter into a greased 13x9-inch baking pan. Bake at 350° F. for 25-30 minutes. Serve warm or cold with the following cake topping, or the "topper" of your choice.

Whittle Street Lemon Sauce

The following zingy cake covering gets rave reviews around the table at our house, at 242 Whittle Street.

* * *

1/2 c. honey
1/4 c. cornstarch
1/4 tsp. salt
2 c. water
1 tbsp. grated lemon peel (optional)
1/2 c. lemon juice

Combine the first four ingredients in a small saucepan. Cook until smooth and translucent, stirring frequently. Stir in remaining ingredients. (Do not boil this sauce.)

Yield: about 3 cups sauce.

Creole Ginger Cake
("Gateau à la Melasse")

Sugar cane is a tropical plant. It was successfully introduced to Louisiana in 1751. The climate is also warm enough for sugar cane in the "Sugar Belt" of east Texas; extreme southern Arkansas; the southern parts of Mississippi, Alabama, Georgia, and South Carolina; and in Florida. Food history buffs (like me) can study early cane syrup/sugar/molasses production by visiting such sites as the Yulee Sugar Mill Ruins State Historic Site near Homosassa, Florida; or the Old Spanish Sugar Mill at DeLeon Springs, Florida; or Laurel Valley Plantation in Thibodaux, Louisiana, with its 72 buildings making it the largest surviving 19th-century sugar plantation in the country.

Enjoy the earthy goodness of cane molasses in Creole Ginger Cake.

* * *

2 c. boiling water
1 tsp. baking soda
2/3 c. molasses
2 tbsp. vegetable oil
2 1/2 c. whole wheat flour
1 tbsp. ginger (yes, 1 tbsp.)

Combine the water and soda in a bowl. Add molasses and vegetable oil. Beat in the flour and ginger. Spoon into a greased 8x8-inch pan and bake at 350° F. for 20-30 minutes. — How about a scoop of vanilla or praline ice cream on top?

Second Helpin' Gingerbread

Recipes for gingerbread date back to medieval England. Originally the concoction had medicinal properties (it still makes you feel good!).

* * *

1 c. cane or sorghum molasses
1 c. brown sugar, packed
1/2 c. melted butter
2 eggs
1 tsp. baking soda
1 c. boiling water
1 tsp. cinnamon
1 tsp. cloves
1 tsp. ginger
3 c. flour

Beat together the first four ingredients. Dissolve the soda in the water, and add the spices. Beat well and add flour. Pour into a greased 8x8-inch baking dish and bake at 350° F. for 25 minutes.

Great-Grandmêre's Molasses Cookies

2 c. molasses
1/2 c. butter
1 egg
1 tbsp. ginger
2 tsp. baking soda
1 c. sour milk
4 1/2 c. flour

Put molasses and butter in a deep graniteware pan. Put on range to boil. Beat egg light. When the molasses and butter have boiled 2 minutes add ginger and soda and take from fire. Stir in milk and egg, and then flour. Beat well. Butter tin sheets and drop batter on them in teaspoonfuls, being careful to leave space for cookies to spread. Bake in quick oven (400° F. until lightly browned).

Wheat Germ and Oatmeal Cookies

Out West, a traveler may be asked to this day if he prefers "long sweetnin'" (molasses) or "short sweetnin'" (brown sugar) in his coffee. — The long sweetnin' in these cookies make them yummy with coffee, tea, and especially milk. I first made them back in 1977 when I operated a pre-kindergarten school in our home. I was determined to give the children more healthful snacks than store-bought cookies or chips. I think the kids were initially a little suspicious of the unfamiliar, non-uniform-looking baked morsels, but it was love at first bite!

* * *

3/4 c. vegetable oil
1 c. cane or sorghum molasses
2 eggs, beaten
2 tsp. vanilla
1 c. raisins or 1/2 c. each chopped nuts and raisins
1 1/2 c. wheat germ
2 c. old fashioned oats
3/4 c. whole wheat flour, soy flour, or rice flour
3/4 tsp. salt
1/2 c. dry milk powder

Combine the first seven ingredients in a large bowl. Sift in the remaining ingredients. Stir until well-blended. Drop batter from a teaspoon (or larger spoon) onto a greased cookie sheet. Bake at 350° F. for 10 to 12 minutes.

Sunny Oatmeal Cookies from Merry Lea

1 1/2 c. whole wheat flour
2/3 c. sugar

1 tsp. baking soda
1/4 tsp. salt
1/2 tsp. ginger
1/2 tsp. cinnamon
1/2 c. butter or margarine, softened
1 egg
1/4 c. sweet molasses
3/4 c. old fashioned oats
1/2 c. sunflower seeds

    Cream together butter, egg and molasses. Sift together flour, sugar, soda, salt, and spices. Add flour mixture to egg mixture. Beat until smooth. Add rolled oats and sunflower seeds and stir well. Drop from tablespoon onto greased cookie sheet about 3 inches apart. Bake 8-10 minutes.

    - Merry Lea Environmental Learning Center, Goshen College, Goshen, Indiana.

So Fine Molasses Cookies

    The following "top-drawer" recipe will delight all partakers.

* * *

1 1/2 c. sugar
1 c. shortening
2 eggs, beaten
1 c. cane or sorghum molasses
4 c. all-purpose or unbleached flour
1/2 tsp. salt
4 tsp. baking soda
2 tsp. cinnamon
1 tsp. ginger

    Cream together sugar and shortening; add eggs and molasses. Mix flour, salt, soda, and spices. Add to creamed mixture. Roll into walnut-sized balls. If desired, roll balls in granulated sugar. Place the balls on greased cookie sheets. Bake at 375° F. for close to 10 minutes. Makes about 3 dozen.

Ginger Cookies

"One cupful of sugar, two of molasses, one of butter; one teaspoonful of soda, dissolved in a cup of boiling water; one tablespoonful of ginger, flour enough to mix, and roll out soft."

- *Aunt Babette's Cook Book, Fourth Edition, The Block Publishing and Printing Company, Cincinnati and Chicago, 1889, p. 329.*

Ginger Wafers

"One cup of butter, one cup of sugar, one cup of molasses, half a cup of cold coffee, with two teaspoonfuls of soda, one tablespoonful of ginger, and flour enough to make a dough stiff enough to roll out thin. Cut with cooky-cutter; bake in quick oven."

- *Aunt Babette's Cook Book, p. 338.*

Molasses Taffy

"Boil 1 cup molasses, 2 teaspoons vinegar and 3/4 cup sugar to hard ball stage (265-270° F.). Remove from heat, add 1 tablespoon soda, 2 tablespoons butter, and 1/8 teaspoon salt and blend. Pour into butter pan to cool. When cool, pull, pull, pull — until firm and light colored."

- *Recipes of the Early 1800's, p. 19.*

A Tug of the Heart

During the 1800's it was a custom among French settlers to hold taffy-pulling parties on the Feast of Saint Catherine, the patron saint of unmarried girls. Saint Catherine died a martyr on November 25, 307 A.D., so on November 25th of each year, the unmarried men and women in the community were invited to the home of an unmarried woman. There the marital hopefuls paired off to pull taffy. Many a taffy-tugging couple wound up wed!

Molasses Popcorn Balls

Messy, but fun! This project takes lots of hands, so call in a gang of kids or friends!

* * *

6 qts. popped corn (unsalted)
2 c. cane or sorghum molasses
3-4 tbsp. butter

Spread out the popped corn in greased flat pans. Meanwhile, boil the molasses to the hard ball stage . Then pour the bubbling molasses over the popcorn and stir quickly with a spoon. Then butter hands and shape popcorn into orange-sized balls. Place on baking sheets to cool.

Maïs Tac-Tac

(This is an old Louisiana recipe.) Use 8 oz. of popcorn "parched to a blossom" — meaning, popped into the typical pretty white puffs. Meanwhile heat 2 c. molasses to a boil. Combine the popcorn and hot molasses "then pour into little paper cases, about five or six inches in length, three in width and one and a half in depth." (You may use paper muffin or cupcake tin liners.) Let candy cool before eating.

- *The Picayune's Creole Cook Book, Second Edition, The Picayune*, New Orleans, 1901, p. 117.

Butterscotch

Give the kids around your house (young or old) a real taste of yesteryear with this 19th-century-style candy recipe!

* * *

2 c. sugar
2 c. cane or sorghum molasses
1 c. butter
1/2 tsp. grated lemon rind

Combine ingredients, then boil slowly until the butterscotch hardens when dropped into cold water (250° - 260° F.). Then pour into greased pans, and mark into squares before it cools.

Shaker Haying Water

At first glance an "antique" recipe for a beverage to drink while getting up hay seems far removed from today's life-style and foodways, but this drink is of interest because of the group of people who created it and their influence on today's cooking and eating habits.

The Shakers, a religious group akin to the Quakers, set up various isolated communities in New England and the Midwest. They espoused simple living habits including a plain, wholesome diet. (There might be a lot more Shakers around today had they not refused to "espouse" each other!) Food was to be eaten in moderation with an emphasis on fruits, vegetables, and whole grain flour for breads.

During the same period (prior to the Civil War) that the Shakers were formulating their ideas (and their wholegrain breads), a man named Sylvester Graham began advocating even more strongly than the Shakers the importance of bread made from the whole wheat kernel. (Sometimes even now whole wheat flour is called Graham flour.) Graham found many supporters including Horace Greeley and Bronson Alcott (father of Louisa May).

Meanwhile, W. K. Kellogg became interested in good nutrition, and began working with cereals to create "ready-made" breakfast foods. C. W. Post and Dr. Ralston (of Purina fame) soon came on board the "cereal train," and the American way of eating was transformed. Excessive, heavy, rich meals of Victorian days gave way to a lighter, more sensible modern diet. Today the health-conscious American is eating more fruits, vegetables, and whole grain breads — *à la* Shaker! Now, here is that recipe for Shaker Haying Water (from North Union Shaker Village, a Shaker community in Ohio active from 1822 to 1889).

* * *

4 c. sugar or 3 c. maple syrup
2 c. cane or sorghum molasses
2 tsp. powdered ginger
2 gallons cold water

Mix and chill.

Conclusion

We have had mouthfuls of fun learning more about the *"Sweet 'n' Slow sweeteners"* apple butter, molasses, and sorghum, and discovering new (and old) recipes incorporating these products. I hope that you, too, will delight in sampling these sweeteners and preparing the recipes presented in this volume. — May all your days be sweet, and slow enough to enjoy!